"A singular vision of surreal violence and grotesque beauty, sung into story by a voice unlike any I've ever heard before, innocent and wise and comic and heart-breaking beyond belief. Patnaude has woven this hallucinatory, multimedia score from the imagery of B horror films, the language of poetry, and the experience of America's abandoned youth. In words the narrator uses to describe the music of his favorite metal band, *First Aide Medicine* "is terrifying to the extreme, yet beneath the singer's garbled, gravelly voice there lie beautiful, primitive, rackety—at times accidental—melodies buried in the stacks and waves of distortion… for those, that is, willing to risk their lives to enter the labyrinth." Be warned: I didn't realize what I was risking by reading this book, and now I am hopelessly lost within it, haunting it as much as it haunts me."

—Jayson Iwen, judge of the Emergency Press International Book Contest, and author of *Gnarly Wounds*, *Six Trips in Two Directions*, and *The Momentary Jokebook*.

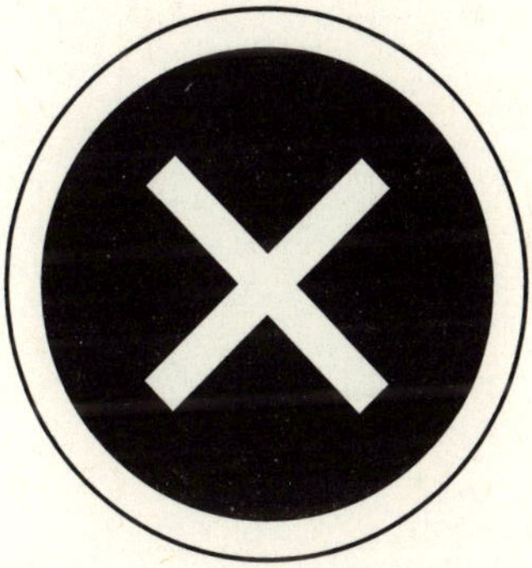

First Aide Medicine

Nicholaus Patnaude

Emergency Press
New York

Copyright © 2013 by Nicholaus Patnaude

All rights reserved
First Edition

For information about permissions to reproduce selections from this book, translation rights, or to order bulk purchases, write to Emergency Press at info@emergencypress.org.

Design by Charlie Potter
Cover art by Tim Lane (timlane.co.uk)
Illustrations by Nicholaus Patnaude (nicholauspatnaude.com)

An excerpt of *First Aide Medicine* first appeared in the *Seahorse Rodeo Folk Review*.

Patnaude, Nicholaus
Fist Aide Medicine
ISBN 978-0-9836932-3-9
1. Fiction—General. 2. Fiction—Literary. 3. Fiction—Graphic

Emergency Press
154 W. 27th St.
#5W
New York NY 10001
emergencypress.org

987654321
First Printing

Printed in the United States of America
Distributed by Publishers Group West

First Aide Medicine

for Johnny & Cabera

"Infected minds
to their deaf pillows
will discharge their secrets."

William Shakespeare

- Prologue -

- o -

Invocation of Karen

I want to burn down his house. I will. He used Karen. I can't stomach that. He was older than piss and uglier than a worm. He lived just down the street with his lights on until late at night. He had an artic fox that turned blue in the summer. But then he had to gouge his kitty's eye out when it killed his pretty blue *Alopex lagopus* one dreary midnight. We all used to go to his curious mansion to escape our prep school and parents. I'm not sure who began the affair, but he was a fox in the snow of Karen's wounded feathers. I call him…then I call him again. I'm driving him crazy with the phone. He's bent over and begging for mercy. If you ever really want to fuck with someone's head, just call them over and over and over again. Soon, I will cut him and run away from his mailbox. Let the blood run down his sides faster than sweat so we can be merry. Cut his life to a flame in a pinch as we await the Ghost Witch's commands in our parents' attics and basements. Why'd you run into a dead man's arms, Karen? You can never escape that crypt alive.

The moss on her gravestone is green and so were her eyes... those fluttering, timid butterflies. Skinny Jeremy and Tubby Rob left, and then Fair Karen died. We two were lovers once, Karen and I. Then the old man crippled her heart with his ancient charms. I throw my trash at the foot of his driveway. I pass by so fast it's like I hide away.

A question remains: Who were you? Who...the fuck...were you? I redial and redial, watching the whites of my eyes turn red. Now it's almost time to say goodnight, old man. Are you there? I've got time to burn and a wistful death-wish for all concerned. Are you ready to change your number?

But it still feels like somebody is missing. It isn't right somehow. Who were you, old man? Maybe it's finally time I took an interest. Who was anybody? Me (Jack)? Jeremy? Rob? Karen? It's all a blur of nightmare fur and everybody has gone and left me a monster. I notice young girls picking flowers off her gravestone; their clean hearts are soapstone. Their small sorrows are for children alone. And all of their stories will never be told. But I need to participate...and communicate. Once upon a time Karen saw somebody nobody else could see. She thought to ask an old man: who were you? Once upon a time I thought to dream of medicine. Now I dream of medicine by the sea.

- I -

My Friends of Medicine

We come from Witchita Falls under the shadows of bat wings. It's a coastal town in Rhode Island where every street is lined with American Elms. I live in a quaint, working-class neighborhood where summer homeowners have the decency to pick up the shit of their dogs from our historic sidewalks. Sadly, it is a lonely town for those of us who live here year-round. The Elms and I grow knotty and gangly with despair during the endless, savage winters. Our bones grow cold and porous. Our hearts sink with the ice-fishermen's sparkling lures to the depths.

BOTTLES surround me. My head hurts. Where is my medicine? I need to sleep the death of vampires. I never thought my jealousy could get this bad. It was Jeremy that left us first. But only Karen can still answer from beyond the grave. This is my one last call and lullaby for this eternity. All of my medicine.

Open your eyes and close your mind. I lie in wait within my parents' basement and listen to the pipes go drip, drop… drip, drop….

Now that Karen has been resurrected, I can travel beyond the black mirror. I can discover who I have lost with the floating hearts and severed heads of my medicine. I must now whisper my other friends back too. I'm sad they're gone…sad and blue.

WHERE did you go, Jeremy? You were another brother in that family—the middle child. I don't see you anymore. Only the blonde girl who was behind you playing with matches—Karen. And I can only feel after her footprints. Feeling travels far when you live with your parents.

I still see your older brother and younger sister. But maybe you just grew up into your older brother. I must release Karen like perfume from a vial…of all the precious times I have forgotten. You…me…Rob and Karen. Our frosted times can still steal me away from here.

I met Jeremy underneath a bridge. It was black night and I'd decided to "run away from my parents" and their television again. I heard somebody chipping at or sharpening something. There were little sparks of blue, white, and yellow. I wanted whoever was hiding in those shadows to swallow me up for good. But who I found was Jeremy, trying to light a cigarette with rocks or flint or various stones. I had matches so we shared that cigarette. It was a True. With the smoke coiling a cobra through my lungs, I finally discovered how to hock a loogie. The world was alive, the sky descending; our times were lullabies and sad goodbyes.

I wish Karen, Rob, and Jeremy still lived here year-round as they did once upon a time. I'd slit my wrists open if it would guarantee their permanent happiness. I stroll on down the boardwalk until I wake up in an alley under the shadow of a yellow spider's legs.

ROB and I had been close since our high school freshman year of pre-season football. Beneath crunching helmets with grass pressing hard against my knees, I struggled to climb out beneath two huge seniors in a drill. Afterwards, I heard him chuckling behind me. I turned.

That was so punk-rock. I could tell right away you were a punk-rocker!"

"Yeah…"

"You're tough, though. Seriously."

He had many freckles and his face had a quality of red as if he'd always just finished a work-out. My legs were sore as hell when we walked up the wooden steps to dinner.

KAREN and I met in a video store. Sweating up a storm, my sickly eyes scanned each overloaded shelf in search of a horror movie I had not yet seen. Our eyes met and locked between the shelves. Who was this girl alone so late at night in search of a faded cassette illusion to disembowel the clocks of time's intrusion? Those eyes belonged to the most beautiful maniac I've ever met. Our love is a vine of entrails that can follow any coffin anywhere, no matter how deep any gravedigger might travel. As I stared at her unblinking eyes, she told me she watched too many horror movies too. I told her, however, that I was nearing the end of my honeymoon period with this microwave of the silver screen; that my reality was becoming too manageable and micro-sized; that the walls were closing in, I said, and I was beginning to have the feeling way too often of having been here before or being already dead. She agreed but tears fell as she said the films were like a balm or a tranquilizer from all the pain. Everyone needs a medicine or a gas mask to make it through this holocaust. My blood in the sky, my blood in the sea: carry me beyond the black mirror so that I may reach thee.

- II -

Goodbye, Aloha

I guess people go in and out of your life when you live near the beach. Ten years ago, when our beach became public, many of our summer friends and families sold their houses away. Then Fair Karen died (suicide) and Chubby Rob left. Skinny Jeremy just disappeared. Like the removal of a sixth finger or extra thumb, my friends are gone. They were the blessed stars of headlight and headlight above the highways of midnight that travelled us so far away from here.

Oh god, why I can't I get my hands on a Jeremy, Karen, or Rob family portrait? Any one? Anyone at all? To see who we all were. A picture that hasn't been folded inward like in one of those trick *Mad Magazine* back-cover pages hiding the fact that Jeremy, Karen, and Rob ever even existed. Even my memories fold to meet without them. Luckily, I know how to pull the corners back and peak inside. They were friends of mine. Nostalgia is a weatherworn ship where I have traveled forever. Regrets are my oars; skeletons, my powder monkeys.

THE LIFEGUARDS are like valentines for summer in their red bathing suits. I'm so glad winter is finally over. The salty sea-breezes reach up to me in my room as if growing and I can smell charcoal burning across the street. I see blood in my fish tank without any fish in it. The water is crystal clear except for the blood. It's just a little cut; no need to alert anybody's sense of infinite danger. It can be just a little sacrifice for the dearly departed friends of mine.

If Karen was here, she'd look at me with concern. She'd tell me to stop worrying about "us"…that my blood isn't a renewable resource…that she and Rob will be here for me forever in memories and dreams. But maybe that would be a lie.

And maybe one winter it will get too cold and I'll forget about the summers we once shared. My family portrait might fold in too, producing the same horrific effect as Jeremy's: that I, all along, had another sibling who eclipsed and became me—a prosperous sibling, an imposturous sibling, who outgrew a sense of time and place in which the three of us were everything to one another. Then only my blood in the sea could unfold and lead me back out of the origami.

- III -

Karen Teeth

Karen would never understand if I told her all about those dates I'd arranged on the beach only to break and sabotage them ten minutes before they were to begin. I am not in a good enough place to commit. I call them from my parent's rotary telephone in the kitchen; I do not have one in my room beneath their basement stairs. They are only phantom girls to me, Karen. They died in a fire when they were little, playing with matches in an abandoned, haunted house just down the street. I always end the spell in time. I'm not afraid. Not as much as who you are in dreams would think. Not as much as the you coming to meet me naked under milky moonlight would think. You wear a wet dress of leaves. I see your poison-ivy bra and hear rattlesnakes. Cobra of my fondness, cheetah blood pumps through my brain.

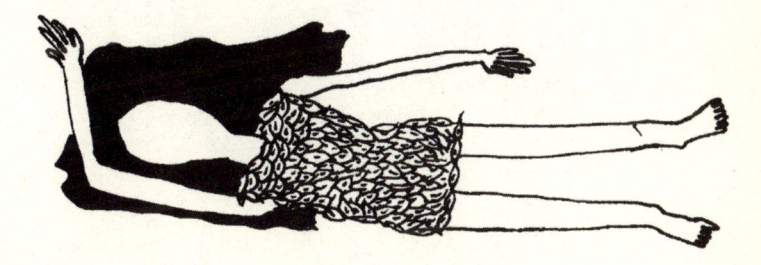

DON'T tell anyone I live with my parents. You lived with yours too. There will always be somebody hiding in us until we move on. Somebody who shouldn't be there. God, but it kills me to know nothing of your true desires. They are ferocious and hiding somewhere, like mine. Karen teeth. Karen has the bluest lungs. I would give anything for an inkling of an insight into the land of the dead.

When I dream of Karen, I dream of damp perfumes. You begin to learn everything you secretly suggested to yourself... everything you always suspected just a little bit becomes blindingly clear and brutally naked: you are who they say you are for a moment and it feels okay. Then you find out the old sluices where you used to hide and disappear have dried up and ejected you. It's the most horrible feeling in all the world. I run upon the boardwalk with the black mirror hidden from all the world beneath my t-shirt.

THERE are lonely cars parked on our street when Karen sits alone. She stares into the darkness of the black mirror at her twin skeleton. She is poised like a Sphinx. She has moved beyond death. I do not wish to walk past the surfboard shop again.

I am a thief God of the night too, Karen. I wish to be blood passing so easily through you, above and beyond you, beating my dusty wings into you. I am a moth made of unused organs the doctors never knew about. I know I could sit beside you, staring into the black mirror, a secret to your parents, a crescent moon to the stars upon your cheeks…or a pair of footsteps in their house they might mistake for old boards creaking away to themselves.

Then no one would ever have to be the wiser about the love we shared; they'd all still just think we were only good friends. But we are the cool sea breezes of the night, skimming above the waves and leaving no footprints.

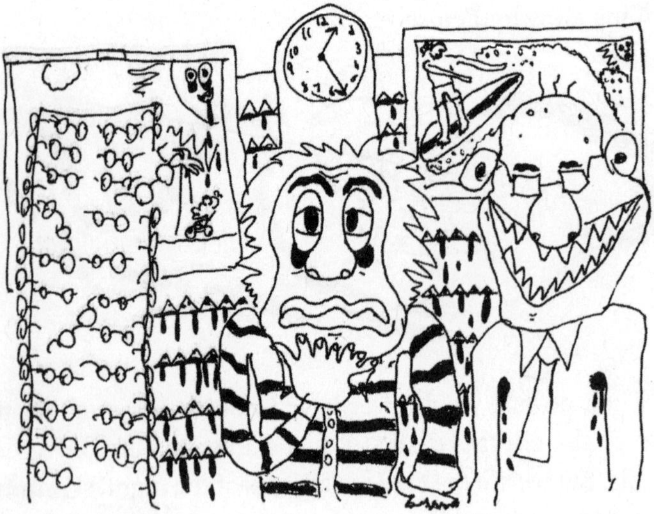

- IV -

Karen Eyes

I have thoughts like this when I'm bored at the surfboard shop. It's misleadingly named for we do not actually sell surfboards; that's just what my coworkers call it to retain a shred of dignity. In actual point of fact we cater to tourists in need of boogie boards and sunglasses with plastic palm-tree rims. I do wish we sold sacred wood to hardcore surfers, but there's another shop for that—of course it's one of those out-of-the-way spots off the main strip that only locals know about.

I have a decade on most of the high school kids who work here. They live with their parents too, but for them it's more natural. How I miss those natural days. There was a time when our eyes shone with promise too, Karen…when simple pleasures like collecting records weren't looked down upon as security blankets for arrested adolescents…but that's really not our final fate, is it Karen? It's like a secret I've been waiting to tell you all day: that I'm in love with you. And so I rush down the boardwalk on the beach to search for the life-guard chair you've been assigned to for the day, ready to tell you something that could cleanse all the blood out of our systems. Yet something stops me each time. It's not that I'm a coward. You just seem to look so far beyond me with your curious insect eyes; inquisitive and alarmed...and frozen in time. Who we once were is trapped in a picture too. Besides, they don't employ the dead as lifeguards.

- V -

Karen Toes

Butterflies made of unused organs could come flying back out of my origami hands. It was like a little gift I gave to myself that I stole from somebody else. I only offer so much as I can stand. I give out signals of disinterest. That's because I only care for Karen.

THE smell of the sea makes me as happy as when I finally approach Karen's lifeguard chair. I see an older, bald man staring up at her like she's a goddess. One of his children buries him up to his neck in sand. What do you see in her, old man? Why do all these antediluvian douche bags want to rip off her panties with their dentures? He stares and stares but Karen is no longer sitting there. It's over old man. She died.

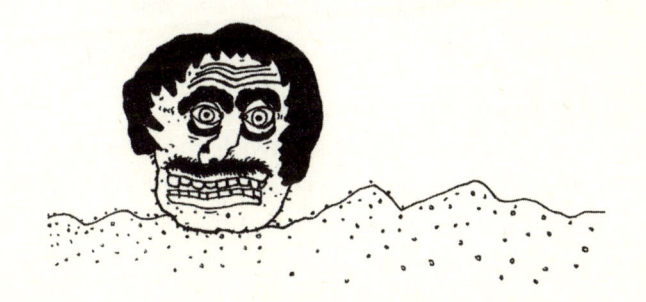

- VI -

Karen Smile

Blood is on a wedding dress. Blood spilt on a tablecloth looks like a carnation. Who's sitting there? It's Karen's family who forgot all about her. Can't they understand somebody is missing? She faded into the background of family pictures until she was part of the wallpaper.

It can happen again, my medicine:
Karen thanks me for the sandwich and we sit on her high lifeguard chair for awhile enjoying the soothing sea and sun. Karen says she's happy with me, but maybe she's just used to me. I remember this summer day with a fondness reserved only for correct dosages.

KAREN smiles when she sees the seagulls. We give them the rest of our sandwiches. We began to taste them, you see. I want to go away with her. But we will never disappear like Jeremy: we have one another in an elemental sense. Just as we know that fire can put out water, also we know that fires can travel underwater for miles and miles.

Karen cries because she used to like movies too. This was before we saw our parents disappear into the wicked blue light. It's a quicksand. Graveyards closing in all around us. You can't be saved if you venture into it with someone you love. Neither mine nor Karen's parents have been to the beach in over a decade. They called all our usual excursions into these nights of infinite danger suicide. But what they didn't understand is that the blue light of these modern dream machines had colored not only their nights but also their days a frozen hue of darker-than-the-deepest-seas blue. Time can never be regained in this fantasy world…or lost.

- VII -

Rob Strong Shoulders

Rob told me about the old man first. Parties were thrown at his curious mansion every night and the geezer didn't care how old you were at all. He didn't care. People his age were already dead, he said. Said the old man to Rob and Karen. We will go, Rob said, but we'll have to crawl home… wink, wink. Rob spoke about his arctic fox, his antique relics, and the derelicts who lounged there. Late at night Old Man Manson walked his fox and talked to it down lonely roads with the tears and fears of a mad scientist or sex-addict who trapped my angel Karen in a blue-glass bird cage.

My eyes glaze over. I believe again in animals without owners. Rob was an army of cousins. A kindred spirit foaming from the mouth of my angel of death.

IT turned out we appreciated many of the same records. He soon tired of football and its rigid practice regiment and became our team's manager—each student at our preparatory school was required to do a sport every season. Being a manager counted. Karen played field hockey. Her teammates didn't care for her; she didn't like breaking a sweat or being in the thick of things. She wasn't a "team player." She'd drift off in the corner of the field, moving offensively forward and defensively backward as if a few steps ahead of the action with a subtly non-committal air. I often chuckled when I watched her games. Did the old man watch her too? Watch her flannel, checkered skirt swaying in the breeze with all the dead leaves while hiding in the prickers with his arctic fox tucked in his coat and his dentures drooling out?

The pain is too strong and I have this craving. I need my medicine time and time again. You see there were so many will-be would-be days when we simply couldn't tear ourselves away from the longing not to go to practice, not to participate, not to risk colds and intense exhaustion because we had something left to give someplace else. Someplace other than those fields… and, you know, I'm not sure we ever got completely away from that need. It was never nourished or satisfied: that need to be the master of one's destiny *without having to participate*…yes, *not* to participate in those activities that made one's intimate soul whisperings a distant echo…how heavenly. Too bad it was a luxury we were never afforded…until now. We wanted to be whole. We didn't want to feel guilt or regret any longer and be the psycho bitch to our imaginary ghost mistress who fucked Jeremy, Rob, and Karen into erasure. And so you'll find us quite at peace with ourselves. Sure, we still have work. It's even worse, yet it's different somehow. The expectations don't haunt us so internally. That's because we don't have careers.

We never will. We are still vagabonds in a manner of speaking: vagabonds of the heart. Life is too slippery to try and stick to....

- VIII -

We were our parents' toys.

Rob used to pick me up at eight in his black van each night. On Fridays, we would go to Phoenix Records with our paychecks and pick up all the new singles and albums. We spent most of our money there and the rest of it in bars. Records gave us a place to go alone. Liquor shook these tall daydreams up into Malibu and coconut bubbles and soon we wanted to lean forward and kiss people again. We only listened to Black Metal. It's the only music I can bear still. I broke every hippy-dippy, positive-vibe Old Man Manson tried to circulate. He lent them to Rob and I broke his compact discs too. His arctic fox must've cried when he saw me sprinkling them by the roadside at the foot of his driveway.

THE clerk with Camels in his shirt pocket always rolls his eyes. I'm back at Phoenix for a drunken stroll down memory lane to burn up my latest paychecks and subsume my being into the unholy spinning wax.
"Don't you ever get sick of this shit?"
No.
"Yeah...sometimes..."
He chews at his toothpick and darts his eyes around.

"You should take some lessons from Karen. She's got the best taste in town. I'd kill to see her record collection. But yours...tsst."

"She died..."

"...I feel like an asshole."

I REMEMBER one of the last night's I ever saw Rob. I sat outside the closed-up shop waiting for him. He was late. It was a warm summer night. I never take the smell of the sea for granted. I didn't mind waiting. I just stood there, breathing the warm, thick, salty air.

"Yo, fuckstick! Ain't you gotta ride yet?"

"Nah, bitch."

The kid had only worked with me for less than a week and he was already calling me fuckstick. He drove a yellow Hummer. Pretty sweet ride, I'll admit.

"You want a ride to basket-weaving class? Huh, ha!"

He peeled out. The sound of it rang in my ears for awhile.

ROB will come soon again. Rob will come back. We'll hit Phoenix Records and then head to The Hut, our favorite bar. I like sniffing the different types of sun-tan lotion underneath the perfume, but it's best when the girls come directly from the beach. I wish Karen could come back too. When she was out with us a lot more girls would come over and I could smell them up close. Too bad she never came out much. Unfortunately, Karen became kind of a recluse—homebody, shut-in, whatever you want to call it.

Old horror movies and T.V. shows washed her windows with blue light. Old Man Manson gave her his entire collection when he was drunk. With dogged obsession, he taped probably every horror movie and creepy, anthology T.V. show that was on from '76 to '87. Sometimes she convinced Rob and me to stay in with her, but we preferred the night-life; we didn't want the death rays of the blue light to bleach our brains to whiteness.

- IX -

Yellow Carnations in the Switching Yard

Twin skeleton saw Karen in the black mirror behind her regular mirror. It has come again, my friends: the time of medicine. The day that time began. I am ultraviolet.

Start the private rituals:

1. Scratch back of neck with fox claw.
2. If no sensation, scratch lower back (erogenous zone).
3. Place resulting blood or skin in baggie.
4. Keep old scabs in separate baggie.
5. Stare into black mirror motionless; become corpse.
6. Introduce fox claw to twin skeleton.

Written in a diseased-like handwriting, I found this weird private torture ritual affixed to the corner of Karen's mirror. I never told her I saw it. Looking up at the sky with her bug eyes, she draws my attention to the purple sunset. I turn as she holds my hand with her cold fish skin. Kissing her is bittersweet. Sangria fangs. Berry mouth. Bug juice. A creature attached to Karen's face is how her kisses feel. Like she is mocking me—overly eager, her tongue probing, her lips sucking forcefully as if daring me to turn away. Rummaging through the cut-up valentine organs in my heart, I feel her dying. She asks me what I want from her late at night when we are alone. Bug legs squirming out of her mouth. Body of blue milk, rippling.

Come back, Karen. Karen, come back.

"WHAT do you want from me?"
"..."
"I have a dark side you know nothing about …"
I recalled the recipe for her private torture ritual.
"We'll cross that bridge when we come to it."
"I'll bring a paddle …"
"We'll row that bridge away from here."
I pictured a bridge submerged in rising water. We began kissing again. We used to talk for hours. I still wear a green lizard leather coat as I drool blood for us: I, the monster; she, the witch.

I never knew what to say. And then she'd give me that fearful look. Sooner or later, I would have to leave her room and walk past her parents' bedroom to use the bathroom. We couldn't stand it any longer, fearful as the invisible eels screaming past us in the darkness. Coming out of rooms with boys or girls or without them, we could never act natural. But we couldn't not act natural. Then again it was too natural. We were over-thinking it. It was already over before it began. There were as many red flags as goose bumps. Millions of warning signs. But we changed each other.

No. No. Somebody had already been here before. Whose corpse lay buried in the garden of our love? The old man's? And so we were afraid to feel anything in case it made a noise. Noises were forbidden before the throne of her parents' martial bed. Waking somebody up might precipitate a downfall into your own shadow's footsteps.

I could never be myself. So then it was like I became someone else. There was someone there but someone missing. We were inseparable. When we took a night off we were sobbing on the phone until dawn. I cried into the rotary telephone in my parents' kitchen above my basement lair. We made love until our bodies were too weak to cross the vast chasm that separates spirit from spirit. We never had to go beyond the black mirror before. Cobras closing in. I was a ghost in her parents' house.

I CAN'T go back to the surfboard shop today. I sit on the hillside above the beach slicing my wrists to give to the flowers all of my medicine.

- X -

The day the red rains dyed
the world to witches' cast

Time still, luckily, to run along the flaming beaches past cooked pork bodies with cucumber slices over their eyes and all the pink and green encrusted beauty masks. We try to work up a sweat and feel some pain before the blue light drowns us in its ghostliness. Body builders with inflated-looking barbells wink at us. Girls playing beach volleyball in their underwear bathing suits blow us watermelon gum kisses filled with jealous venom. It starts to rain. Nobody leaves. Karen is still dead. The corpse of her ghost holds my hand instead. We run faster. Beyond the black mirror.

Immune to the charms of the sun, black circles bloom under our eyes. We fail again to communicate with our hearts. And so they roll down into the sharp tip of the sickle moon. We kiss gently. We are friends. We are no longer friends. We are something else, not something more.

IT was only a matter of time before the old man offered her a refuge from all the static illusions. There was one last straw. There was broken glass and red wine smeared on a new white couch and her mother's bleary, accusing eyes as we stumbled through the doorway…for the last time…and then I passed the shoelaces of her father's work-boots tangled and fraying, never to be welcome. Karen was a damsel in distress I could not save. Then the geezer found her with his searchlight, but I can find him with merely a candle in the blackest night.

Old Man Manson, you cannot hide. There is still time to:

1. Bang nails through his eyes to his brain.
2. Cut off his arm then make him eat it.
3. Rip his skin off and staple it to his back like a cape.
4. Make him drink gasoline then jab a syringe full of fire up his ass.
5. Piss into his face then smash a bottle over his head.
66. Kill him.

- XI -

We came from Leafy River to the throne of the Ghost Witch.

We don't want her parents ever to see us. What time should I leave so as to completely avoid them? I'm not sure. They keep catching me. Sneaking up on me…even when they're not there…even after our love lies braided with cobras and buried in Karen's grave. The eagle with his eye hanging out by a goopy thread is the shadow of his own death, or so said Karen about her own life. I creep into the lampshade dawn to sell some sunglasses.

First Aide Medicine

I RECALL a summer night when we all were still together. Rob finally came to pick me up after I'd been batting bugs and listening to my thoughts in the dark for a while. He was late because Karen agreed to come along at the last minute. Anyway, she just had to finish this one T.V. show—she claimed the suspense was killing her. That's exactly why I step outside the blue light.

"Rob said you'd be pissed ... I'm sorry."

"Ah, don't worry about it."

I was happy she'd come along. It's not like we'd miss any of Blue Smoke's set or anything. Blue Smoke was a Norwegian black metal band that happened to be playing at The Hut that night—mainly because Rob and I were devoted members of their fan club and he agreed to put them up.

Rob had his own place. It wasn't much, but it was his. *De Mysteriis Sathna*, their debut LP, hadn't left my turntable for over a month. Maze-like, their music is terrifying to the extreme, yet beneath the singer's garbled, gravelly voice there lie beautiful, primitive, rackety—at times accidental— melodies buried in the stacks and waves of distortion... for those, that is, willing to risk their lives to enter the sonic labyrinth.

Karen moved to the back of the van and sat on the couch beside me.

"What's wrong?"

"Nothing."

I was thinking about the old man again.

"No...what is it?"

"Sick of work, I guess."

"Yeah..."

"I just never thought I'd end up someplace wishing for the days to end..."

"It doesn't have to be like that."

Karen looked unbearably beautiful when she felt hurt. A dim but steady tenderness poured from her eyes. I leaned in to kiss her, but she gave me a brief hug and pushed me away. She untied the shoe-laces of her Converse All-Stars and retied them over and over again. I wished we were in her room making love or strangling the old man until his eyes popped out.

I grabbed Karen's hand and kissed it, but she only retreated deeper into her shell.

Karen cringed as Rob ran over a few metal trash cans.

"Oops."

I wanted Karen to smile so bad that I traced one around her mouth with my fingers.

- XII -

Yes, They Love The Inventor.
Love his long, white hair.

Blue Smoke's set was phenomenal! Even Karen agreed afterwards—she said she never realized how "avant garde" black metal could be. *De Mysteriis Sathna* was played from start to finish at a blistering pace ending with a cover of Accept's "Losers and Winners." The blue vinyl I'd spun countless times ticked against my heart, emitting blue sparks and smoke from a cauldron of dreams. Of course Karen would've preferred David Bowie or Iggy Pop, but people like that never come around here.

ROB gestured with his hands and spat as he talked to the members of the band.

The turnout hadn't been bad. I'd like to think I had something to do with that. Hell, I'd spent the last week plastering flyers to every telephone pole I saw for miles.

The van ride back to Rob's was quiet. Were Blue Smoke too stunned by Karen's beauty or just too tired to talk? Then again maybe their English simply wasn't good enough. Didn't matter. Soon enough Rob and I were chattering up a storm, singing their praises, and talking shop about other Black Metal bands.

The singer was much smaller and more nervous than I'd pictured when listening to *De Mysteriis Sathna*. When Rob dropped me off at my house, the singer became warm and friendly, getting up to see me off and putting a hand on my shoulder.

"You tree might stardt yohr own bahnd?"

I hugged the guy. He blushed as he hopped back into the van. Karen stared at me through the tinted window. As the black van drove off, her glare of hatred or sorrow remained like a scratch from an arctic fox across the windows to my soul. It was the last time I ever saw her alive.

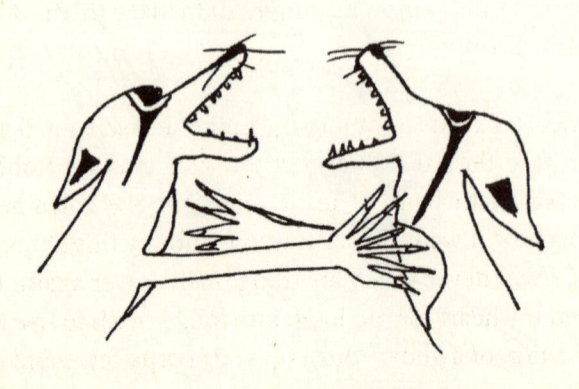

- XIII -

She is the black angel whose pockets overflow with severed heads.

I sorta regretted not going out to party with Blue Smoke, but they seemed pretty tired. Rob's place would've been too cramped for me to sleep there anyways. Besides, I can barely sleep when I'm not in my own bed—whenever I do, it makes the next day way too dismal to handle. It wasn't the drip drops of the pipes calling me back to my lair beneath their basement stairs; sometimes I just need to be left alone. And my parents never talked to me…staring at the throbbing screen, their lives grown mean and distant…Karen and I lived in sin and stumbled in…we walked so far beyond them…and whether Karen was coming or going simply didn't faze them. But not that night. No, not that night.

KAREN'S head rolled into the gutter and screamed at me. I didn't have the axe. Who held the axe? Jeremy? Rob? Her father's prosthetic hand? The old man? No. She killed herself. That was how it went. It was freezing and my fingertips grew blisters. I will never watch anything on T.V. ever again. It has poisoned my heart for too long. I no longer wish to live life as the reflection of a ghost. Open up your corpse eyes and come back to me, Karen.

Graveyard of graveyards, does the Ghost Witch let Karen come near her with her downcast eyes and morose expression? Lava trickled down the walls of her room. Her parents were fighting again. Her parents were fighting. Her father kept yelling that, "I am not yelling." Then they talked. They weren't throwing chairs, but somehow talking was worse. It weighed too heavily and never let up.

"You spent too much money on that prosthetic hand," her mother accused her father.

Her mother guilt-tripped him.

"The hook-hand was perfectly all right. Your hook-hand made you a person everyone could understand, but your fucking prosthetic hand with bionic fingers is drowning us in debt. And now nobody can count on you!"

Karen fell into the sea of despair in her black mirror behind her regular mirror.

"No, we're broke because of our pathetic daughter and her 'friend.' I can't go on working pro-bono for a pair of drunks. I am no longer a 'hook-man.' Now I have a hand!"

Karen smoked Dunhills. Her eyes turned black. She couldn't go out. She looked up at me within her sheets, shivering with fear. We both knew it was the beginning of the end. Nobody I've met wants to live anymore.

- XIV -

We knew the toucan bird clock could watch while our bodies made friends.

And then another day passes with the usual tourists coming into the shop for boogie-boards, sun-block, and sunglasses. I watch the clock painfully inch itself towards twelve o'clock. Its hands are dying worms. The past can never pass. Blood drips from my fangs.

I decide to take lunch early.

I walk along the boardwalk with two grilled cheese sandwiches filled with jalapeños: one for me and one for Karen. A European girl wearing a green bikini shaped like mint leaves is fast asleep beside Karen's high lifeguard chair. Karen looks like someone had stolen her soul across the night. She is rotting much too fast. Her eyes are black, vacant windows to hell.

"Climb on up."

She eats the sandwich in almost one bite.

"You have to remember to eat more."

She burped lightly.

"I know."

Karen keeps her eyes pretty much glued to the ocean front as I eat my own sandwich—she takes her job more seriously than I do.

"Not too crowded, huh?"

"A shark washed up earlier. A dead one."

"Yeah?"

"It sent everyone running for the hills."

I couldn't believe my good fortune. I scanned the beachfront eagerly for a glimpse of its carcass.

"Was there much blood in the water? Did any of the lifeguards with the blood-red bathing suits get blood on their legs?"

She smirks.

"No. It didn't happen like that exactly. Some park rangers came in a van and lifted it up wearing these black rubber gloves…kinda like the shark was radioactive or something."

First Aide Medicine

"Weird."

"Yeah."

Karen often tells me about odd stuff she sees on the beach. All she ever does is gaze and gaze from so high up. She gives me a curious smile. Her teeth fall out with a waterfall of maggots. I'm not sure if she knows. She knows her mother eats so much candy that root-canals are routine, but does she know about the night of imaginary knife fights and shadow fires...the night when my nightmare married my monster in her mother's bedroom?

IT is the night of wickedness of which I speak: 'twas a winter eve cold and bleak. Karen and I drank too much on the porch and then stumbled toward her bedroom doors. Her father was away and her mother was afraid. Half her face was hidden away. The shadow of a hook-hand upon her wall meant somebody was there even though nobody was there at all. My blood boiled. My teeth were falling out soiled. My blood grew hot pink. Her blood: a hard red candy drink. The hook-shadow gripped in anger more or less. Gripped and shredded her gummy dress. Her white curtains fell behind her hot red gums. Her unused organs beckoned me to come. My mind was burning. My teeth were falling out in curtains.

KAREN sits on her lifeguard chair decaying too fast. Like time-lapse photography when flesh turns to nothing but bone...cold, hard bone...and now some other lifeguard sits in the chair where she belongs. She was a good friend to have. I wouldn't trade anything for once having her in my life.

Before I knew it, my lunch-break was over and I had to hustle back to the shop.

- XV -

And then I got visions of this white wolf through all the imaginary moments of Karen's infidelities. I recalled her past. She recalled her past. What's passed never passed.

I thought about that dead shark a lot the rest of the day. I wish I could have been there to see it. Had its corpse flooded the ocean water with fresh blood? I drew a picture about it with some crayons from under the counter on one of Roger's (my boss) old menus. Lifeguards swarmed around it with fresh blood on their legs. It matched their red bathing suits. The half-limbs of many unfortunate beach-goers floated level with their chests.

I drew Karen on top of the shark, dressed like an Amazon woman, and stabbing a spear into its heart. She wore a necklace with many real skulls on it. I drew her that big. It would have made a great cover for our album if Rob, Karen, and I had ever ended up forming a metal band like the lead singer of Blue Smoke once suggested.

THERE was almost no business that afternoon at the surfboard shop. I began to pray that someone, anyone would make the bell on the door ring. I wanted to disappear. I wanted to die. The spirit of Karen was crying out to me somewhere far away. Couldn't our lunches like those happen over and over again like repeating a favorite song? Eventually, I fell asleep.

I walked down a long, black-and-white-tiled hallway in an apartment complex. Karen's mother lived in the penthouse, but you couldn't get up there without a special elevator key. She had black, shiny hair so long it almost touched the ground and wore a peach-colored nightgown made of gummy candy. She looked just like Karen's mother only younger.

"Have you ever been to the curious mansion before?"

She continued past me.

"Old Man Manson wants to have a talk with you."

The ceiling above this hallway had many steel beams. There was steel grating on all the walls.

The elevator was already waiting for her.

"I'll slip inside this blue glass noose."

Its door was open and there were two people inside it: Karen's father, who was dressed like a general and had hooks for both his hands, and another person who did not resemble a person much. The monster had a lot of fur: white on his face and red and black striped fur everywhere else. There was something pressing outward from inside his stomach. Fur grew uneven there and the face of a boy moved under his blotchy, grayish skin.

"Aren't you coming along?"

On the ride downstairs, Karen's mother's shiny, black hair got tangled up in one of Karen's father's hooks. She thrashed about. Then her hair got stuck in one of the elevator buttons. The elevator bell dinged upon reaching the lobby. The furry creature removed a knife from behind his back and chopped Karen's mother's head off. As it rolled away, the hair got tangled up in knots. She raced after it as it rolled through the elevator doors, the lobby, and, finally, the building's front doors—which the doorman opened for it. It stopped when it got outside. Karen's mother followed it then paused too. There were no other buildings around except for a tower. We were in a clearing in the middle of a forest. Karen's mother bent down and picked up her head by its hair as it spat black blood and mumbled:

"Behind you runs the Ghost Witch through these summers to beyond the black mirror…"

Karen's mother turned and saw an old man wearing only a t-shirt tangled up in a pricker bush. It was Old Man Manson—the geezer Karen had slept with. Karen lay tangled up there too except she was more cut up and dead. Although flaccid, Old Man Manson's penis was large. My teeth sprinkled out like snowflakes. The black and red striped creature helped Karen's mom cut Old Man Manson down with its knife. The monster looked at me with devil eyes and drooled.

"When you sleep with a corpse, all the green leaves turn black."

Karen looked so sad. Old Man Manson ran away. Pieces of his ripped t-shirt fell like a trail of breadcrumbs behind him. The Ghost Witch was standing before the tower. She had a key in her hand and was about to unlock the door. The tower was made of slate. The Ghost Witch turned the key and the tower collapsed into a neat stack of double-sided axe-shaped pieces. She looked back, waiting for me. Her breath was as cold as Karen's heart.

IT was at this point that I heard the bell on the door clang. I realized I had been someone in the dream too. I was the one who was supposed to have killed Old Man Manson.

The red and black-striped creature was disappointed. He had been waiting for me to kill the geezer, but I hesitated and so he cut the old man down. I drifted away to greet another customer.

- XVI -

Invocation of Karen the Ghost Witch

Karen, fly upon your broomstick across darkened skies the witches cast. I cannot hate or love you anymore with my true skin flying so high above me and out of reach. The stars are caving in. My grip is slipping. The pipes above my basement room are filled with blood. Hairs sprout from me everywhere. My fangs have grown and I know for sure I have eaten people before. Kill me, Ghost Witch, so that I may walk like a zombie into the land of the dead and be with Karen forever one everlasting time. The red and black stripes can paint over death's oblivion. My shrunken head tastes blood lipstick and all the unused organs. We are together again at last: Karen is the Ghost Witch.

I call Karen. I invoke Karen. It is our one last resurrection. I recount my dream from work.

"Why would you make something like that up?"

Her voice sounds deep and gravelly. Does she have laryngitis? No, it is because she is dead.

"I didn't. It was a real dream. What do you think it means?"

Silence.

"—YOU—OVER?"

Her voice keeps cutting out.

"Huh?"
"DO—OVER!"
"DO—WANT TO SLEEP—!"
Her voice keeps cutting out.
"Karen? … Karen?..."
"—SLEEP OVER?"
Her voice sounded like Attuchka (the lead singer of Blue Smoke) when he summons the devil in "Foggy Funeral."
"DO YOU WANT TO SLEEP OVER?"
I wish I hadn't called her. My head fills my blood. The blood boils my veins. My fangs grow hairy with diseases. I'm losing sight of them all. My eyes are falling out. My teeth are falling shadows.

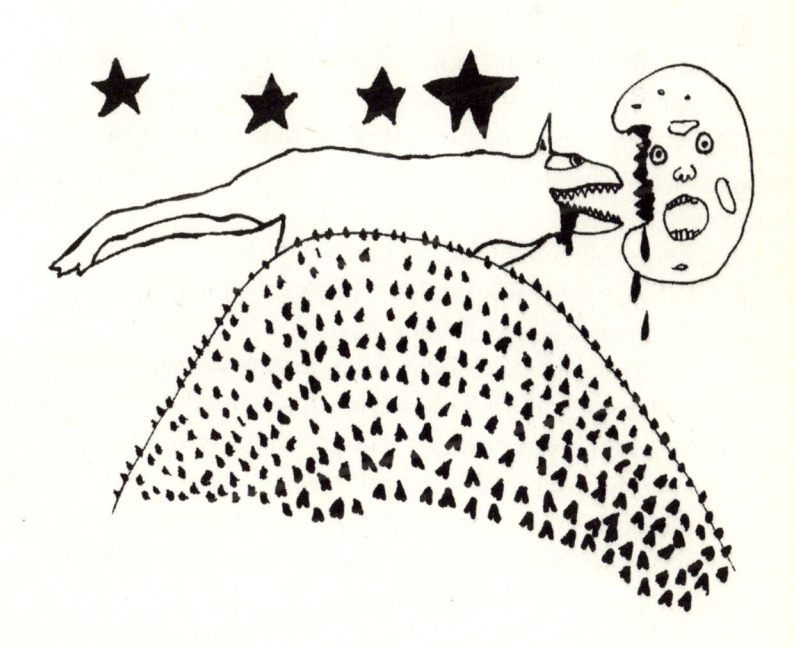

- XVII -

It smells of burning sulfur in my basement room: something's wrong with the family furnace, I guess. So long have I despised these winters.

I swim for miles with a razor-blade in my swimming trunks. I just do a little cut now and again to attract the sharks. Nobody can see me way out here past the blue buoys. I wish a shark would come and eat me. I might even put up a good fight. Or maybe I'd just give in like Karen did to Old Man Manson.

The people are so far away upon the beach. They have no idea of anybody way out here, licking the blade of suicide. Seagulls squawk above me looking for fish.

I don't have to work today or tomorrow so that probably means I'll head to the bar if I survive this swim. Pull down the curtains and cover your eyes. I'm growing tired of treading water and there are wolves in my eyes.

I wasn't always this much of a monster, just as Karen wasn't always this much of a Ghost Witch. We once had innocence on our side…just like everybody else.

I remember the days fondly when Rob, Karen, and I were freshmen in high school. We used to sneak out. We were usually up to no good…but in hindsight, it was good…good as a dead goody two-shoes. Sneaking away at night really lit us up alive. Wandering through graveyards, sneaking into churches, and skinny-dipping in the ocean way past midnight, we drank handles of the bluest ocean waves and felt brave and irresponsible. We were the night salamanders the waters never burnt.

THERE were occasional difficulties escaping under our parents' careful watch so we rigged up a Walkie Talkie system for all our night-time tactical maneuverings.

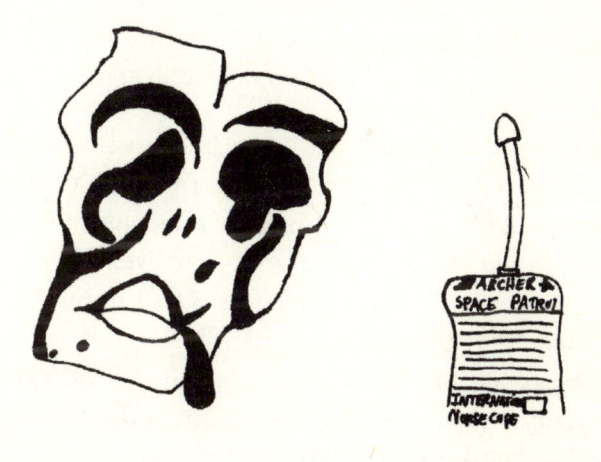

I recall one night after we'd radioed one another when we sat on the ledge of the town swimming pool; it was a place a lot of people went for a dip to wash off the salt from the ocean. I remember the water felt a little bit cold that night. Rob had a band-aid on his knee and I was afraid it would fall off. I wondered what a lot of blood would look like in the swimming pool and if it would form into the shape of a wolf—that really seemed beautiful to me, a wolf made of blood running along the bottom of the swimming pool like a blood shadow.

I also remember the way Karen was dressed that night: she wore these big, hot-pink hoop earrings; a bracelet made of bamboo and sharks' teeth; and a pair of Honolulu-colored boys' swimming trunks that hid her purple bikini. She'd brought along a couple of mangoes in her see-through, black, holey beach bag. She ate one as if it were an apple.

Something slammed loudly with violence. It came from a changing-room shack at the corner of the pool. A big, gray, weatherworn piece of plywood was affixed to the shack upon which had been written BOYS and GIRLS in red with dripping red arrows beneath. The color of the red paint was the shade of my blood.

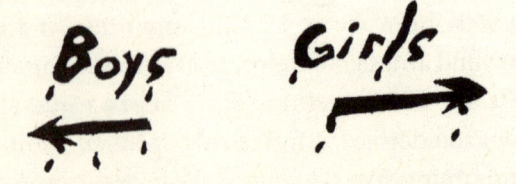

First Aide Medicine

Rob pushed against the plywood with all his might. Nothing happened. He grew tired and stopped. Then Karen tried a different approach: she pushed at the top of plywood then wiggled it loose with her fingertips. The board wobbled. Then she got a splinter and stopped.

"Ow!"

I grabbed her hand and removed her splinter with my teeth. I spat it out as if I'd just sucked out the poison from a snake bite—and then she gave me one of those looks. Rob sweat like he'd been under a heat lamp for awhile. He had a zit in the center of his forehead that was about to burst; it looked like a third eye. I wanted to pop it so bad. After the pus and white goo was ejected such a lot of blood would fly out…it might even be in the shape of a wolf too.

It was my turn. I gave the top of the plywood one hard shove, felt some weight give, and jumped back, narrowly avoiding the bottom from scraping my shins as it began swinging around and around. Rob grabbed an old cinderblock from beside the shack and tossed it beneath the spinning plywood. The cinderblock landed in its path and stopped the door from spinning. We stared into the darkness beyond.

Then, in a fury, Jeremy (who I hadn't seen in months) squat-ran onto the jammed board with a sling-shot pulled back, poised and ready to shoot. Nerves might've made him fire the rock. It whizzed by Karen's face, almost grazing her cheek, and knocked one of her pink hoop earrings clean off. Poor Karen: she had already gotten a splinter and now a stream of blood ran from her ear to her shoulder blade. I hated myself for wanting to lick it up, but the sight was as dazzling as blood upon snow.

Jeremy dropped the sling-shot and Karen ran to hug him. He appeared angry and hardened. His skinny back heaved with sobs. Dark circles under his eyes.

"I'm sorry. I thought you were somebody else."

Jeremy offered Karen a white handkerchief. A stain of blood soon blossomed throughout its perfect whiteness.

"You guys shouldn't be here…"

"Jeremy?"

Then Rob knocked Jeremy out with a rock.

Rob stood over him. His hand holding the bloody rock was shaking. I bent down to check Jeremy's pulse. He was still alive but Rob had scared me.

First Aide Medicine

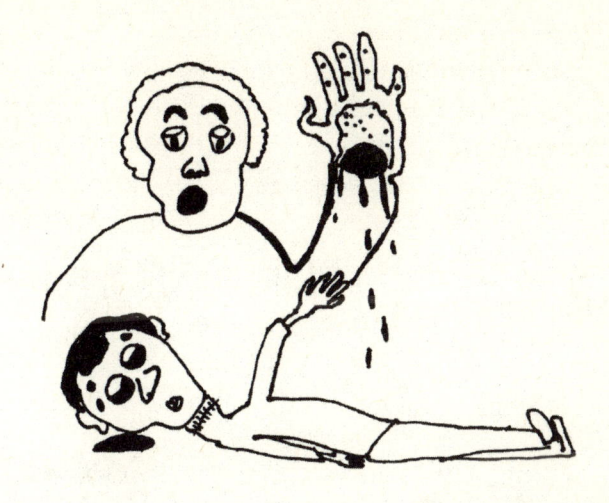

Jeremy's blood was a brighter red than Karen's or my own. My eyes darted from the blood on Jeremy's forehead, Karen's blood on Jeremy's hankie against her ear, Rob's bloody rock, and the painted BOYS and GIRLS upon the changing-room shack with the color shade identical to my own blood.

We helped each other over the wobbly piece of plywood. It was hot and dark inside. Rob and Karen's breaths felt close. There was peach fuzz on each of their faces. Upon the ground was cool, soft dirt. It grew cooler to the left so I went there. Karen grabbed my arm, losing her balance. Her body buckled forward and we fell onto a soft material that made my eyes itch.

- XVIII -

Firebird blinks in the chocolate darkness.

I looked around. We were in a barn. The door was open and there was a lock and chain hanging from it. I soothed and eased Karen and Rob out of their tense positions until they snapped out of their trances.

I walked over to the barn door and peeked outside: we were across the street from the public swimming pool. My vision became pressured from all sides. It seemed so simple in appearance: all we had to do was walk across the street to get back to where we were before, but it was all different now. It was like I could never completely return to who I'd been. Who...the fuck...were you? Rob and Karen looked outside, but then they touched their temples sharply and sat down. I ran my shaking hand through my long blonde hair. The hay on the floor felt itchy. I wanted to rip off my sweaty skin. The room spun and my temples throbbed like jackhammers. We could never find our way back out of the origami again.

I heard somebody breathing too fast...hyperventilating. It was Rob and Karen...and me. I shouted Jeremy's name between shortened breaths. Had he disappeared here? But who the fuck were you, Jeremy? Honestly now...Jeremy? We got so lonely. It's why Karen slept with Old Man Manson and our relationship was tattered mummy bandages fraying in the wind of our parents. I became monster. She grew so much afraid.

Pieces of hay scratched against my eyes. Rob and Karen wriggled in a cloud of dust, their faces blue. Jeremy's bloodstained handkerchief lay under hay.

Jeremy leaned against the barn door, his sling-shot in one of his belt-loops, fresh blood on his forehead, and bits of cakey, dried Karen blood in his sandy brown hair. The barn began to revolve. There must have been some sort of embedded axis beneath it because all Jeremy did was lean. He never took his eyes off me. His face was pale and powdery and there were stitches around his neck.

- XIX -

The Dirge of Genie Disappear

And then on that last summer evening the four of us were ever to spend together, Jeremy told me a story:

"I used to sneak out...I couldn't stand listening to my parents squabble night after night after night. I went through the shack and ended up here too. Only...somebody else. There was a shark with gray, human-shaped legs bent over like a hunchback. It smelled of radioactive chemicals. I could barely breathe and the room was spinning. He wasn't happy to see me. I reached out to him. He hissed that he could help me but at a price. Will you consent? I nodded. He spun the barn around like I did for you. He told me I must guard the door night after night, day after day, and never be seen or I would die. And so that's where I've been all these years."

"At first I just stood near the shack, afraid to go inside and face that awful sickness again. But I grew bored and went in. It was dim. I could see a dingy sink, a refrigerator, and a grimy lab table. If you walk to the right for about a mile, you will come to two large doors. They lead to a narrow alley that empties into a domed football stadium. All the lights were on. My eyes were blurred. The stands had been overgrown with exotic vegetation. The enormous score board was an antique. I got a burst of energy and ran laps. The air was clean and fresh. I approached the fifty yard line. Then I saw him on my left."

"The hunchback shark held a football between his fins. He threw me a screamer and I ran it into the end zone just for the hell of it. He motioned me over with a fin. He cradled the football against his human-looking gut...like a beer gut.

'You've been doing a good job,' he said, placing a slimy fin upon my shoulder.

I thanked him but complained of the seclusion, loneliness, and futileness of the endeavor. He took his fin off my shoulder and fondled the football. His breath sounded unhealthy as he hunched over.

'You never have to come back again if you do this one thing for me,' he said.

There was something gummy and red stuck between his sharp teeth. I worried he might ask to suck my blood.

'Just stick your hand through my leg for five minutes.'

His stumpy right leg had a horrible-looking gash in it. There were green inch worms and pink earth worms crawling around inside it. I stuck a finger in. He leaned back in delight and his eyes rolled to whiteness.

I left one finger in and counted down the minutes.

'The five minutes starts when you put your whole hand in.'

I pried apart the wound and thrust my fist inside. He nodded like it was okay for me to start counting. The gash moved. It suction-sucked and massaged my hand so hard against my knuckles I had this fear my fingers were being rearranged. I was afraid they'd crawl off my hand and stay inside him forever. I yanked my hand out.

He wept. I looked at my hand. My middle finger had moved. It was now next to my thumb. I ran back to my post."

That's how Jeremy's story had ended. My friends are still gone. All of them. I want them back too: let this be an invocation to all of you. I feel terrible without roots. I am a stranger in this town. I am Frankenstein's monster.

I return to The Hut.

"Get lost, you fuckin' disco stick!"

I hadn't heard last call. I rarely heard it. Jackhammers pounded in my brain for some more to drown my soul… to strangle it into submission…why didn't I know anyone around here?…who can you talk to?

I have to wake up and work at the surf board shop in three hours. My tears are sparkling stars. The bartender will miss me when I don't come back. I can hardly stand up, my Princess Devour.

- XX -

The Banjos of the Navajo Snake Charmer's Corpse

It becomes too dark when I step outside. Only Karen's face is pale moon bright.

My memories are alive. My thoughts are burning. My teeth are falling out. My memories are talking to me. My memories are talking:

"Why'd you run into a dead man's arms?"

I wanted to drink her blood. There wasn't anything else to drink.

"He bragged all around town about what he did to you."

"…"

"How could you fuck that old man? Did he give it to you good? Huh? Did he?"

I want to rip his wrinkled face off. I am a massacre.

"Did you ever go down on him?"

"No."

Karen's voice was murky…echoes crossing over from the land of the dead….

"Did he go down on you?"

"He tried, but I said no."

I wonder who went on top. I picture condoms in his bedside table drawer. I picture him shitting on an antique john the next morning as she lies in bed, hungover as all sin… she buries her eyes in the crux of her elbow.

"We were drinking buddies…he was always trying…and then one night I gave in…and…then I went back…again… and again…and…again…"

"He stole your life."

"Not my life. Your life."

"Huh?"

"He never meant anything to me. Nothing to me at all. Only you."

- XXI -

The Fox blew frostbite at the cemetery.

I'm losing control of my thoughts right now. I'm losing control. It's been three days since my last confession. I got thrown out of the bar last night. I'd blacked out until some hardcore douche bag had me pinned up against the railing out front. The doorman helped him throw me into the alley. My thoughts are growing frosty. Morals become lazy if left unexercised. My face is scraped up and black-eyed. Without temptation comes damnation. I feel better now but always like a few hours have just passed below me.

MY parents made TV dinners again (big surprise). I try to stay in with them and watch television. Then I remember again, my medicine, the haunted look in Jeremy's eyes, and the cakey-white stitch scar around his throat. I remember the old man and I remember Karen.

The droning of my parent's television becomes unbearable. The canned laughter echoes through my brain like a feedback loop…even when it isn't there and they turn on some "slice-of-life" HBO or Showtime show. We are not really living through these television characters' lives. These are not real experiences no matter how racy or controversial. I can still hear it in my basement room. It grows louder and louder. They think it's funny when I suffer. They turn it up on purpose.

I leave through the basement door.

I wonder when my zest for life vanished as I wander around town. I can be reborn. It doesn't have to be over yet. Maybe I can find a new Karen.

The dream I had when I slept at the shop feels too distant. I wish I could go back and look at it like an enchanted observer at an aquarium…like Karen once did…she never told me the secrets behind it…

I go back to the pool and open the changing-room shack but Jeremy does not jump out with his loaded sling-shot this time. I hear somebody inside crying.

"Jeremy?"

I freeze up.

"Jeremy? Is that you?"

I peek inside. The hunchback shark is engaged in trying to jam emerald and ruby rings over his fins. Several bent rings lie beside the sink. I should run.

"Yeah. It's me, Jeremy."

"It can't be! You're…you're…dead."

He runs off.

It smells of ghastly chemicals. A green glowing substance had been spilt here and there. I find a beaker filled with blood on the ledge of the filthy sink. I lean in to inspect it and knock it over. I watch the blood in the sink. It is much thicker than ordinary blood and remains where it splattered. Since no one is around I lick it up. Nobody will ever know about that.

I follow Jeremy's directions to the football stadium. It isn't as lush and verdant as he'd described. It is like a ghost town and everything is dead. There are about 100 or so animals' skeletons scattered all over the field. Cobwebs cover the massive lights, only about half of which are working. I sit on a stump in the middle of the field and stare at the half-collapsed wooden stands for awhile. The dead vegetation reminds me of that dried-up fish flake food...the way it floats on top of the water.

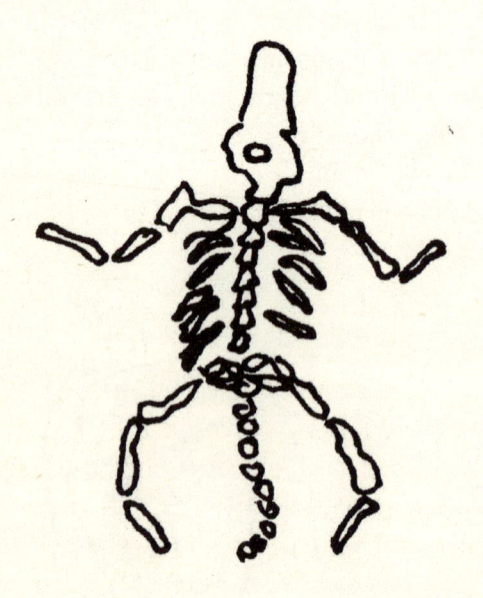

- XXII -

We dance with dinner suits in the shadow of two horns.

It always used to go this way: sitting in her car with cigarettes and ultra-light beers during winter months; talking about her nightmares and my nightmares; the heat on at full blast; the past never passed. Karen wore the old man's coat. We shivered and looked through the frosted windows at her parents and my parents. When would they go to sleep? We waited chilly until the clock turned black.

BRRRRING…Brrrring…Brrrr—
"Hello?"
It's Karen."
She was in a bad state tonight. She cried and she cried.
"You'll meet someone someday and love will change you, Karen. You'll see."
"But I'm already dead. There's nobody else here."
"Then you must be an angel, Karen. Yes, Karen is an angel."
"I wore a peach-colored nightgown when the creature followed me home to my penthouse apartment. He was waiting for me in the elevator."

It is horrible to talk like this. She is almost done bawling her eyes out. I have to hold the phone away from my ear for a while during the loudest parts. This is my first phone call from beyond death.

She continues sobbing.

The line starts cutting out. Her voice becomes distorted, deep…screechy. It becomes the disembodied voice off a black metal record sans instrumental backing.

Her voice keeps cutting out.

- XXIII -

Karen is an angel.

Her voice keeps cutting out. I look into my closet mirror and see the monster staring back at me. It's starting all over again, but this time it can happen differently. We are angels from the land of the dead plucking all the rotten apples from the past and sprinkling our medicine. Her voice comes back into focus.

"I sing in my sleep. I went back there where the black and red-striped creature trots. The old man got stuck in the pricker bush again. His huge dick pointed straight up. He was crying because he was stuck and bleeding in the pricker bush."

"You had blood all over your mouth and a knife in your hand. I remember the old man climbing back up into the pricker bush...acting like he'd done nothing to me at all... nothing to me at all...but he fucked me...it wasn't rape...I let him...I even went back to him again...but I wish I could take it back...he had an artic fox for a pet that turned blue in the summer...that was the only thing I ever found beautiful about him...then his cat killed it so he had to gouge his own kitty's eye out..."

"Karen?"

"He is crying in pain for me to come and save him. My parents are the size of children."

There is static. There is so much static that it is howling.

"Then it's like I pick the old man off the pricker bush like a piece of fruit. I want him to stop when he hugs me too tightly because he is fucking me when he hugs me. He tells me he invents things and he's even more precious than a princess. The decapitated woman's head glares at him when he says this. It is my head. Black blood continues to dribble from my head's mouth. I try to put my head back on my body but it doesn't fit."

"The black and red striped creature sits on top of the pile of slate, double-axe pieces of the tower. He scrambles down in a mad ape rage when he catches me looking up at him…His horns cast an awful shadow. He killed me when he followed me home that night…me…the crazy girl…the stupid one who went and got herself decapitated by the blue glass noose. I turned blue in the summer just like the fox. He followed me up her stairwell when I was so drunk after work that Friday night. He hated the old man as much you do. And he looked like you when you get so angry. Rob had just dropped me off after the black metal show. His fur was so bright it made the dark seem only like pretend. But his red and black fur had streaks of blood in it…"

"Karen?"

The line goes dead.

- XXIV -

The radioactive shark who scratched tropical tattoos

Karen looks like she didn't sleep. That is because she is dead. I can't tell whether she is a walking corpse or a ghost. She sits way high up there on the lifeguard chair, her hand guarding her eyes from the sun even though she wore sunglasses—it isn't merely another hangover this time. Can you still drink in the land of the dead? I wonder if anybody else can see her. She takes off her sunglasses and I see the white maggots crawling out of her eyes. Karen is the Ghost Witch for all remaining time.

I climb up and hand her a BLT on rye. She wears pink lipstick encircled by a light green…even in death, she is still so guava.

"Did you dream again?"

She nods her head. It tips back and almost falls off. Maggots writhe within her slit throat.

"I went back into the same dream. Only this time you and Jeremy and Rob were there too. There was a smoldering, smoking campfire. The naked old man from the pricker bush squatted over it. It was like his water had just broke or he'd just peed like a girl. Black blood still trickled out of the long, black-haired woman's decapitated head who looked like me. It was now impaled upon the General's hook-hand. It was like something else had happened when I was away…like if you get up to go to the bathroom during a movie or miss an episode of a T.V. show."

I begin to grow a little anxious. I was due back at the surf board shop ten minutes ago.

"We knew we had to walk away from the house and the stack of slate, double-axe shapes that had been the tower. The woman's head on the hook led the way.

'East, southeast, and northeast,' she shouted

I noticed General Hook's ghastly mustache. It appeared fake and as if covering a terrible wound. I didn't want to get too close to him. I knew the woman's head would bite me.

After an hour or so, we reached a juncture on the hilly dirt road. The black and red striped creature followed us, hiding behind bushes and trees whenever we looked back. He wanted to stay a secret from us. He wanted each of us alone in the dark, dark woods.

We went down a steep hill. A stretch of the road ahead was flooded as deep as a river, but it wasn't flowing or moving at all. There were fish swimming around frantically through the dark waters. The fish were vibrant, fluorescent, and glowing. General Hook was stumped. Rob sweat bullets, gasping for air.

The corpse of the Ghost Witch (who made the tower come apart) floated by. I jumped in the water to prove I wasn't afraid. But then blood poured out of your mouth. I rushed to the other side and the blood flow lessened. Then you, Rob, Jeremy, General Hook, and the naked old man from the pricker bush swam across. The red and black striped creature peaked out from behind a tree at the old man. The old man had many red ants crawling all over him. There were so many that he didn't even look naked anymore. I could only see his eyeballs and pupils through the swarm of ants."

The flesh around Karen's corpse elbows began to blister in the sun.

"The red ants didn't hurt him so we continued down the hilly, dirt road. The forests surrounding this road grew thicker. I looked back at the red and black striped creature. He looked upset and abandoned.

'East-West,' the woman's decapitated head spat more than spoke.

I ripped the head off the hook and threw it in the water. The water froze and turned pitch black. The red and black striped creature did an acrobatic jump onto the woman's head frozen in the black water and then another onto our side of the shore. Everyone grew uneasy. General Hook ridiculed me for disposing of our "guide" (the decapitated woman's head).

Up ahead, the road ended. The forest was too thick to continue. I tried to proceed, but it was like pushing against a stack of sticks standing upward. Then the ants upon the naked old man from the pricker bush did the strangest thing: each tiny one prayed, pulled, and leaned toward the too-thick forest. They climbed upon the shoulders of others until all were standing, stacked-up on one side of the old man. They had formed a shape like a steeple…or an arrow. He was still naked except for this steeple or arrow of ants that grew and swarmed out of his side. I didn't want him to think I was staring at his dick, so I looked away. And then you grew angry with me. You walked over and slapped me for doing it. You kept following me around the creature, trying to slap me again. He growled at you.

The creature looked to the thick, thick forest. Then he removed one stick at a time from the forest wall. After a half-hour he had barely made a dent. He motioned General Hook over, grabbed his hooks, and struck them together like flint. Then he signaled you over and mimed how blood came out of your mouth before and asked you to spit some more on the hooks. An explosion went off when you did it. A deep hole was burned through the thick, thick forest. There was now a crawlspace…like a tunnel. The man from the pricker bush was covered in soot from head to toe. The ants were blackened too and appeared dead.

First Aide Medicine

The black and red striped creature crawled into the hole first. I called for him and he scrambled backwards. He extended a back leg and paw. It looked like a lucky rabbit's foot, but his claws were so sharp I screamed. He retracted them. I grabbed his foot and he pulled me. I told someone else to grab my foot. We could form a chain, I said. You went next, then Rob, Jeremy, General Hook, and, finally, the old man from the pricker bush. The black and red striped creature was so strong that he pulled us all pretty fast. The ground was cool, smooth…like the dirt underneath a rock, so it didn't hurt. That's where last night's dream ended."

- XXV -

A cunning fox avoids the wandering bullet.

"Thanks for walking me home. It's been such a spooky day..."
I wish she would put her sunglasses back on. The maggots' children's children begin to emerge from her empty eye-sockets and mouth. Her rotten stench makes me puke.
"Ewww...god...are you okay?"
"Yeah..."
Death is the worst smell of them all.
"Do you want to sleep over?"
"Sure."
"Don't be nervous or anything. My parents really like you."
Karen's eyes bug out and she begins hyperventilating. Her left eyeball falls into my palm as softly as a grape. I want our blood to mix together; our drinks together; our dreams together. I hold her instead.
She pushes me away and begins to weep.
"Don't look at the shadow of the horns upon my wall. We will never have sex again if you see them there."

We get under the covers with our clothes on, too nervous to sleep. I fight the urge to kiss her. She leans over and onto me and turns off the light. She takes her clothes off and so do I. Time passes but her breathing doesn't change so I know she is still awake. There is enough moonlight spilling in through the window. I can see her milky back and worry that her parents might burst in at any moment and find us naked like this. They might think I dug up her grave…they might even convict me as a corpse robber….

And so there was never really a moment of peace within our parents' midst. Their routines and histories were so deeply rooted and ingrained within the house's fabric that their spirits were forever present in every room. And so there was always someone else. Someone there but someone missing. I am a monster in the pale moonlight wanting to chew her milk flesh into all the bloody bandages, at one with the mummies and the vampires. Fur sprouts from my face. My fingernails grow wicked. The walls offer no protection against her parents' threats. Every boy and man she'd ever slept with was with us tonight too. Not just the boys and men but the way her parents saw these boys and men—the hyperbolic Halloween mask versions of these boys and men who stole their daughter's heart and mind; and I am just another one too, perching over her in my carrion deathskin deathmask. I see the shadow of the horns upon her wall. I know she will remain true to her word: this is the last time we will ever sleep together.

Her body is a cold mass of bloody bandages, hacked-up flesh, and white maggots about to explode from gluttony.

"Why am I such a monster? What happened to me?"

I hold her tight.

"It can happen to anyone."

"It didn't happen to you."

"Yes it did."

Then she hovers above her hacked-up body; she, the sad Ghost Witch.

"Why the fuck did you leave me for that ugly old bastard! He was practically a corpse when you slept with him!"

"I had to get away from my parents...from your parents."

Karen flies like an angel.

"He offered me comfort at a time when nobody else could. Not even you. You were just so goddamn heartbroken all the time."

The lower jaw of her corpse-body falls to the floor. I hold the rest of her corpse head, never to be decapitated again.

I wonder how we did it together. How did we manage to travel back and forth between our parents' houses? Our love was eternal then. It could withstand anything...except...I retain a hatred for Old Man Manson. I am sleeping with him too. I am sleeping with the devil. I am danger. I am destruction. I am the mutant the parents had to shield their pretty little kiddies' eyes from.

It's felt like nine thousand years since my last confession. It hurts to remember her so much. It hurts in my teeth, which are falling out like tears. And it hurts in my eyes, which are falling out like tears. And it hurts in my heart which comes tumbling out like one giant blue tear Karen might mistake for the blue topaz ring I once gave her.

MAYBE if we'd wandered outside naked and in love things could've turned out differently. Someday soon we'll travel beyond the black mirror. It can happen today. Right now.

- XXVI -

The last runner's velvet horse

When we get outside, we are not on the street but on the floor of the apartment complex where my first dream had begun. The woman with the long black hair now looks like Karen and Karen's mother combined. She is someone there but someone missing and she is no longer decapitated. She wears a dress made of a gummy material colored rainbow like gummy worms. She exits her apartment and walks towards the grated elevator without noticing us and presses the call button.

We stand beside her and wait as the elevator rises up through all the levels of beams and grated walls. General Hook (who now resembled both our fathers), the red-and-black-striped creature, and Jeremy are waiting in the elevator when the doors open. The woman's hair gets caught in an elevator button, but we manage to disentangle it before she is beheaded. The black and red striped creature holds his knife aloft for the remainder of the ride, poised and ready to decapitate.

The lobby of the apartment complex bustles with activity. It is like a hotel. New guests come and bellboys diligently stack their luggage. Well-dressed gentlemen talk on ancient telephones with detachable ear-pieces, many shiny keys on rows and rows of hooks behind them. The floor of the lobby is a peach-colored marble. Around its perimeter sit cocoa, marijuana, and tobacco plants. Though we can hear waves crashing and see and feel sunshine bursting through the large windows, we are back at the clearing near the tower when we walk through the front doors of the apartment complex.

The old man in the pricker bush howls in pain, wearing only a shredded white t-shirt and bleeding more than the first time. His penis has also been greatly shredded by the prickers. Maggots crawl among the wounds. We do not rush to release him. I hold Karen back. Tears rise in her eyes. I am the one who is supposed to have killed him. I have this monster inside.

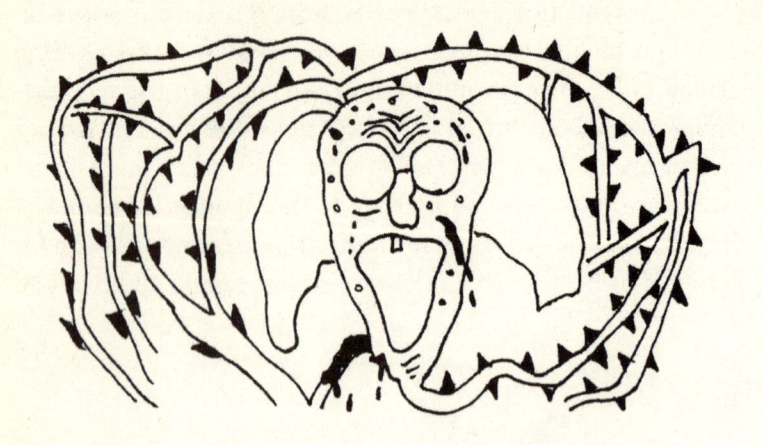

I grab Karen's wrist as we rush over to the tower to guard it from the Ghost Witch. I can hear women crying from atop the tower.

"Help! Fire! Fire!"

I see no fire or smoke.

The Ghost Witch arrives punctually and ignores us. She pokes her key directly into Karen's belly button. She gives us a perplexed look. Her cap blows off. She hides a lot of bluish-tinted black hair under there. It is as long and silky as the woman's in the gummy dress. It blows freely. Then it gets caught in a hook of the General. He decapitates her with one swift pull. Her body walks away unfazed.

Out of the corner of my eye, I see the black and red striped creature climbing up the side of the tower at a rapid pace. The screams of the women in the tower become more ear-piercing and horrifying than before. I try the door. It is locked. We run to the other side of the tower to help.

There is a gray wooden deck near the top of it. The creature has slaughtered six women dressed like princesses. Severed legs and arms flop on the floor and hang on the railing. He holds the head of one in his furry hand and eats her face. He eats with his mouth opened. He has the worst table manners in all the world.

We hear the screams and moans of the old man in the pricker bush again. Karen runs to help him. I follow her dully.

We look over our shoulders and see the black and red striped creature scaling down the side of the tower with the elegance of a spider. I want the creature to eat the old man for dessert. Karen works on disentangling him, panicking at what my love might do to him and her.

The prickers on the bush are nail-sized and the color of almonds. Pierces and punctures from them speckle his body like chicken pocks...or many bees could've just stung him. His grayish, wrinkled skin looks even more disgusting with all those gashes in it...like a piece of meat, butterfly cut years ago, then dropped someplace out of reach to rot. He keeps crawling away from us, further into the depths of the bush. I chuckle. Karen grows angry with me. She doesn't want to see him to suffer.

The creature is nearing. She pulls Old Man Manson out by his ankles. He falls onto his face as a branch swings out from under him and stabs my thumb. It is not exciting to see my own blood in the least. I wish Karen had been the stabbed one. The creature stands by us, his eyes glassy and hungry at the sight of my fresh blood; his white-furred beard is red with gut-hangings and blood to the roots from the devoured princesses. Kissing him at that moment would be sweet tart. I bet him I can eat the old man's face quicker. I restrain the tiger inside me.

The creature starts coughing then crawls over to us and lies on his back at Karen's feet. Little fists punch up against the skin of his stomach, stretching it so we see the grayness of his skin beneath the black and red fur. A child's face rises up... and another face...the face of one of the princesses or very fair maidens...these faces pressing up against the creature's stomach's skin howl mutely in desperation.

Something begins hitting at a metal shutter in the turret window of the tower's attic. Then the steel shutter falls down with an awful clang that rings in my ears for a solid minute.

A cat climbs out and crawls onto the roof with a knife.

Once upon a time Old Man Manson gouged his kitty's eye out when it killed his arctic fox. His kitty is back. Karen is back. And it is only here that we can work through our undead sorrows.

Karen picks up her child-sized parents, carrying them tucked under her armpits. I am the one who's supposed to have killed the old man by now. I am supposed to cut him and run away from forever.

- XXVII -

Slipping the panther a slipper of dancers

"Follow the toadstools and come back to my house."
It was the witch's head who spoke. General Hook cradles it.

Karen's child-sized parents want to go home "this instant." Each holds one of Karen's hands. They are helpless.

Tiny fists and howling faces no longer push up against the black and red striped creature's stomach. He lies as still and forlorn as if he'd just vomited. Now he is too sick to eat the old man. General Hook paces back and forth. He keeps glancing at the sky and listening to the Ghost Witch's head whisper him things. Then he gets upset and wanders down the road…just as he'd done in Karen's dream. We all follow. I hope we are not going to the home of the Ghost Witch.

We come to the flooded place in the road. I look back and see the cat with his knife chasing after a toad.

Karen holds her trembling parents' hands as they gape at the painted fish in the water. The woman with the gummy dress dives in, rises up, and leisurely backstrokes. The fish congregate around her and nibble at her gummy dress. She pets them.

I swim across. The old man follows suit. Karen's parents hold onto her shoulders as she swims. When General Hook enters, the water around the Ghost Witch's head begins to bubble. She cackles as bolts of lightning shoot out from between her sharp and crooked teeth through the water. I hear a cracking sound as though from somewhere deep within a frozen pond. General Hook scrambles up onto the other side, leaving the witch's head behind. Karen is still held back by the weight of her parents as the water becomes blackish and frozen. I tug her hand with all my might. Her parents slip off her, sink under the water, and become still. Her tiny parents are frozen in black ice. Karen claws and claws at the black-ice block and weeps. I do my best to console her. Then the creature catches my eye. He looks at the ice uneasily. The Ghost Witch's head sinks and then freezes upside down under the ice with a frozen surge of lightning issuing from her cackling mouth.

"Don't worry. It's frozen. Come along."

It was Karen talking to the black and red striped creature in a sing-songy voice. I know she loves this monster more than the monster in me. He walks quickly on the ice upon the tippety toes of his claws and collapses after he gets across, his body a swarming mass of red ants. He shrieks and runs down the path, through the thick, thick forest. We jog after him. The woman with the gummy dress is in front of me; many fish still cling to and nibble at her dress.

I hear an explosion up ahead. We reach the too-thick-to-proceed part of the forest Karen told me about. There isn't a hole; instead, there is a tunnel shaped like a cut-out of the creature with his arms held aloft and his legs poised in mid-stride.

I feel an intense wind at my back. The sky darkens. We have to walk with our legs spread-eagled in order to fit into this creature-shaped tunnel. I let everyone else go first. They have to wiggle and squirm in order to slide forward into the creature's imprint.

Before I ease myself in, I look back and see the cat sitting on a stump eating toads off his knife. A flash of recognition passes between us like I am about to do something he approves of and wishes he could do. Something evil…criminal. Chips from our shoulders will chip his heart to crumbling pieces. I would have to kill the old man before dawn…before he put his boots on. Our hatred of the old man congeals to form a single, infinitely-toxic, airborne unity. It begins to hail. Thunder sounds. I fit myself into the creatures shape and wiggle after the others.

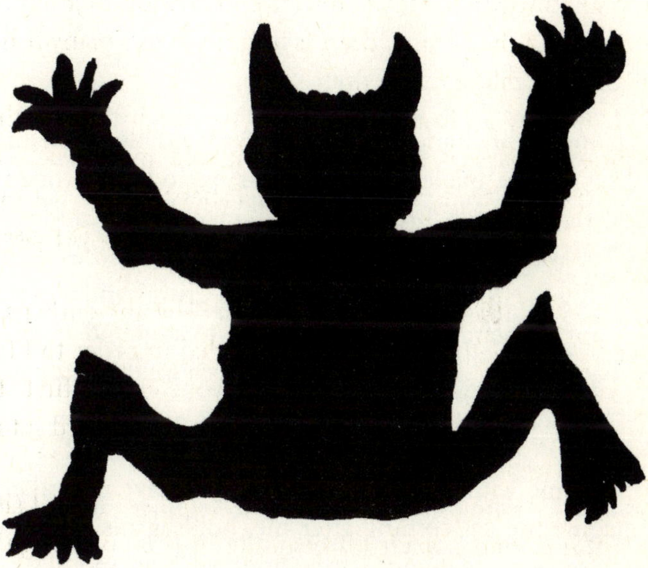

- XXVIII -

Hoof prints in the emerald garden

It is incredibly dark and quite uncomfortable in the tunnel the creature made by burning or exploding through the thick, thick woods. Broken sticks scrape my spread legs as I crawl. I wish I wasn't last. The cat with the knife might be following me. Judging from occasional grunts and whimpers, I am not far behind the others. I have to stop and stretch my legs backward while leaning forward because they keep falling asleep.

I feel disheartened and weak. My blood no longer rushes through me with its usual fluidity. My resolve is weakening. I imagine the cat coming after me, holding his knife to my back. It keeps me going. I grow uneasy horns and black soul fur slashed with streaks of blood in stripes.

First Aide Medicine

I smell a cigar (an expensive one) and the smell of sweet nuts roasting. The stones lessen and then I crawl out onto warm, slippery leather.

Karen is there beside me on a couch so huge I fear we've shrunk to her parents' size. We're in some kind of huge inn. I know that because of the enormous staircase. But there are red and white toadstools outside. I see them through a stained-glass window. This is...the house of the Ghost Witch. It must belong to Karen now.

The whole entourage trots down the stairs in their pajamas: General Hook, the woman in the gummy dress (now wearing a gummy nightgown), Rob, and Jeremy. Oh, and the old man from the pricker bush finally dressed in quite debonair, playboyish pajamas that would've been a smash at breakfast after an all-night ball or bash in the 1920's.

They all stop mid-way down the stairs and begin whispering secrets. The secrets are about me and Karen. A burst of flame erupts behind us and we cast huge shadows upon the entourage. I turn around and see the cat roasting toads on his knife in the fireplace. He wedges it like a spit between the stones. On the mantelpiece are Karen's parents still frozen in a block of black ice that is beginning to melt. Karen rushes over to it. The cat winks at me and makes a stabbing motion in the direction of the old man while Karen's back is turned.

"It's melting, Jack. It's actually melting!"

Rob slides down the banister.

"Have you guys seen your room yet? My god, it's huge! Attuchuka's upstairs sleeping off some jet-leg. Ours is pretty sweet but I think you got the best one in the house—the honeymoon suite! Sorry, I couldn't resist sneaking a peak. C'mon, let me show you!"

First Aide Medicine

I follow him as he joyfully bounds up the stairs two at a time. Before he can open the door, the dinner bell rings.

"I guess the room will have to be for dessert."

I wasn't looking forward to the roast toad but even that might taste better here.

We go into the dining room and find the creature with the black and red fur upon the table instead. He has an apple in his mouth and there is no sign of the red ants. He doesn't appear cooked though…not even seasoned.

The cat leaps upon the table and stands with great poise and concentration, his paws neatly folded behind his back. He frowns at our trepidation upon seeing the entrée.

General Hook lunges at the heavily garnished creature, slicing evenly from his Adam's apple to his waist with a hook. The cut widens smoothly. The heads of the six princesses or very fair maidens and the head of a child rise out of it upon stalks the color of peas. Each head then gracefully lands upon one of the seven plates before us.

General Hook, the woman in the gummy dress, Karen, me, Rob, Jeremy, Attutchuka (who just joined us and who sat side-saddle upon Rob's lap), and the old man from the pricker bush all raise our knives and forks ceremoniously and begin to carve at each of our allotted heads. In Rob and Attuchka's case, Rob holds the knife and Attutchka, the fork.

As the skin and skull of each of our heads parts and widens with the ease of the skin of a peapod, it is, perplexingly, not brains that we were greeted with but strawberries, cream, a rose, and a dove, the last of which coo amiably in unison.

The contents of our skulls are too ornamental to be devoured, nevermind the fact that the doves are likewise uncooked and the combination of goodies therein are more like living sculptures than edible dishes. It doesn't matter. I am not hungry in the least. None of us are. Base and nasty thoughts like that don't trouble us here.

The old man from the pricker bush is the only one to receive a dead dove. He pokes it. The cat massages his chin with his paw with a perplexed air then winks at me.

The black and red striped creature turns his head on its side and stares directly at Karen with a look of pain. His eyes blink slowly. He is still alive but the horrible wound must've weakened him. Karen was his last soul on earth. But even she betrayed us.

I hear a horrible squawking. General Hook is trying to behead his dove with a hook; he jabbed it in the side of the dove's long neck. He pulls at it as if it were a hook stuck in a fish. It rips and tears until the head is off and the squawking stops. General Hook leans in quick and slurps at the bubbling blood from the dove's neck. That would sure be a fun way to kill the old man!

Large, blue tears form in the corners of the creature's eyes and hang there thickly like sap. Then his lips come together, forming a small o, and he blows a sound like there is a beer bottle below his lips. Then his eyes close and the creature passes away.

The cat walks upon the table, offering his knife to help dice up the live doves. We refuse and eye our meals as though at an art exhibit. General Hook makes a swipe for the cat, presumably to behead him, but the cat swiftly side-steps out of harm's way. He is near me. He breathes heavily and emits a strong and quite human scent of musk.

"Should I wait until you've killed the old man or should I bring out dessert now?"

I nod.

"Now?"

I nodded again.

- XXIX -

Flower dents in the pink soap sidewalk

The cat pushes in a dinner cart while walking on his hind legs. It bears a magnificent ice sculpture representing two swans shaking water from their wings. Then I look to its base and see which block of ice he'd used: it's the one containing Karen's small parents. They had moved though. Whereas before they were hovering in its center mid-swim, now they lay upon the bottom with their arms crossed and their eyes closed.

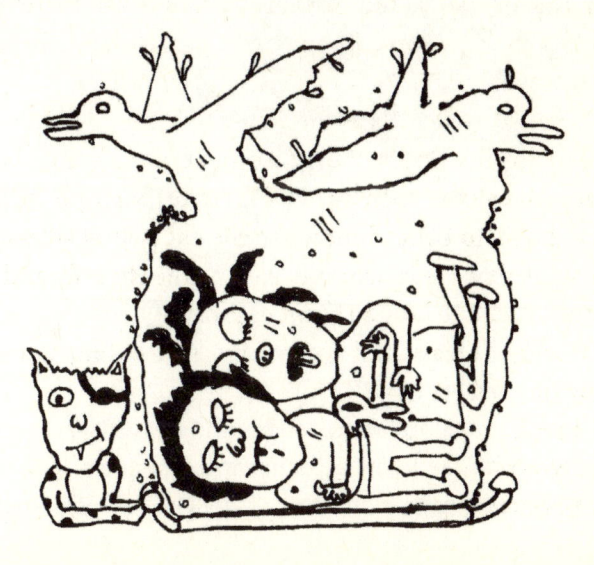

Karen pushes my hands off her lap and begins to weep embarrassingly loud. The cat stops pushing the cart and looks at Karen's outburst with curiosity. General Hook rises and attempts to decapitate the ice swans, yet both his hooks snap off in the endeavor. He backs away in horror, staring at his precious hooks stuck in the swans' necks. There is a tiny area around each implanted hook that has cracked. Beneath each area, tiny drops of red blood begin to fall. Blood not only runs down the sides of the sculpture but also inside of it so that a cloud of moving blood gradually obscures Karen's parents from view. It is the shape of a wolf.

It swims and hovers and speaks to me. It tells me it is now time to kill the old man. I put the black and red striped creature to shame. I eat the old man's face and head so fast I spray bits and chunks all over the cat. I chew with my mouth open. I have the worst table manners in the world.

The cat, visibly upset, steers the dessert cart out of the dining room. He turns a corner too fast and the cart begins to tip. Karen leaps up and rescues it. The two airborne wheels

First Aide Medicine

slam back down upon the black and white checkered marble floor loudly. She picks the wiggling, squirming cat up by its neck. It struggles for breath. I cry out for her to stop. Then there occurs a silence so long I think there is something wrong with my ears. My eyes are stained with blood…someone is turning up the red. My ears are blood shadows, my horny violence.

- XXX -

Epilogue

Years pass. We return to Karen's funeral again and again. I follow the looks of the mourners into the ground. I follow their eyes and I follow their tears. It scares me that her father doesn't have to be polite to me anymore.

Our memory grows hazy of you, Karen…we can no longer remember what you look like. The human brain can't do that after a while—it can only let go.

We grow dumber and hungrier as the years pass. We drink more. Have fewer ideas. Become more perverse and wretched.

Our memory grows lazy of you. Hazy of you. We are cold here. There is too much time.

I TAKE a leak behind the surfboard shop after smoking two cigarettes in a row. Impatient customers stare at me when I return. My mind just wanders as I ring up the pointless sales.

I walk along the beach on the way to her grave during my next break. I picture Karen rotting beneath the earth. White maggots crawling out her eye sockets. Maybe she can dig her way out of there again someday soon. Maybe right now.

I can't seem to return to the surf shop alive anymore.

I'm scared to be quite honest. And I'm totally alone, despite Karen.

Late in the night, I turn on my side to escape the lung-poisoning stench of death. She's over there awake…awake and undead, yet not quite a zombie or a corpse: she is as beautiful as a vampire.

Maybe the funeral was just some charade, like the moon landing. We begin drinking ourselves into oblivion outside my parents' basement crypt. I walk through her piss. Her blonde hair is the color of piss and smells of freshly-killed cobras. The yellow spider stretches across my brain with the cracking of a crystal ball.

I only remember fingering her in the shallow river after that—her blonde hair thrown back as she buckled in gratification, sewing our seeds into corsets and corsages. The rushing river massaged her anus and my anus. It was the perfect temperature for skinny-dipping after midnight. Late summer. Bottles of red wine and aged whiskey floating away. Together alone at last. Yet some devilish monster fast-forwards this pleasure to its inevitable climax too soon. Unto infinity. But then maybe we overheat every television across the world. Goes out and breaks the tube or whatever powers the pieces of shit.

I WAKE beside her gravestone in tears. I wake with a thorn in my foot and terrible poison oak bubbles around my ankles.

My parents are away, yet I stay alone in their basement crypt. I've told their dogs this was no longer their home. They cried and cried the first few days, pathetically whining for food and shelter. But now they've found someone else's bones to pick.

SHITTY internet dating sites match me up with trolls as I cough and sneeze from the mold in my parents' basement. I'm getting the fuck out of this little town filled with ghosts and losers. The antidepressants are no longer doing the trick. Then I realize I am not alone.

Someone else is upstairs. I'm too scrawny and wasted to put up much of a fight. I fear him taking my place at the table. I fear him making my remembrances impossible. The floorboards (my ceiling) creak again and I feel it is the last straw for this horrible person sent to replace me. The footsteps don't have the patience to wait and are too delicate to be a dog's.

Perhaps the footsteps upstairs merely belong to one of my parents' friends…or to a caretaker, rearranging tables and chairs to avoid the disrepair of my basement crypt. And then it could turn out I was listening incorrectly all along…that all this sadness and dread were a pack of phantoms and mirages.

THE mourners at Karen's funeral look murky from down below. It's like looking up from the bottom of a swamp.

No amount of danger could ever bring us back together again, Karen. There are footsteps all over my seasick heart, and I am retching as the boat rocks. What a little white lily got burned along the edges and fell in a porcelain sink.

BRRRRRING...Brrrring...Brrrr—
"Hello?"
"Hello my boyfriend who is dedicated, obsessive, creepy, and sweet."

Acknowledgments

Thank you to Bryan Tomasovich, Jayson Iwen, Tim Lane, Charlie Potter, my teachers, my students, my family, and my friends.

The production of *First Aide Medicine* was supported by the Antioch Media and Publishing Center in Seattle.

Emergency Press thanks Leah Rae Hunter, Frank Tomasovich, and Jill and Ernest Loesser for their generous support.

green press INITIATIVE

Emergency Press participates in the Green Press Initiative. The mission of the Green Press Initiative is to work with book and newspaper industry stakeholders to conserve natural resources, preserve endangered forests, reducd greenhouse gas emissions, and minimize impacts on indigenous communities.

Recent Books from Emergency Press

Farmer's Almanac, by Chris Fink

Stupid Children, by Lenore Zion

This Is What We Do, by Tom Hansen

Devangelical, by Erika Rae

Gentry, by Scott Zieher

Green Girl, by Kate Zambreno

Drive Me Out of My Mind, by Chad Faries

Strata, by Ewa Chrusciel

Various Men Who Knew Us as Girls, by Cris Mazza

Super, by Aaron Dietz

Slut Lullabies, by Gina Frangello

American Junkie, by Tom Hansen

EMERGENCY PRESS
emergencypress.org
info@emergencypress.org

Nicholaus Patnaude grew up in haunted, rural Connecticut. After completing his degree at Bard College, he worked in a variety of mental institutions and halfway houses. Currently, he is a teacher working in Istanbul.